A Note to Parents

For many children, learning math is c
math!" is their first response — to which many parents silently
add "Me, too!" Children often see adults comfortably reading
and writing, but they rarely have such models for mathematics. And math fear can be catching!

The easy-to-read stories in this **Hello Reader! Math** series were
written to give children a positive introduction to mathematics,
and parents a pleasurable re-acquaintance with a subject that
is important to everyone's life. **Hello Reader! Math** stories
make mathematical ideas accessible, interesting, and fun for
children. The activities and suggestions at the end of each
book provide parents with a hands-on approach to help children develop mathematical interest and confidence.

Enjoy the mathematics!
• Give your child a chance to retell the story. The more famil-
iar children are with the story, the more they will understand
its mathematical concepts.
• Use the colorful illustrations to help children "hear and see"
the math at work in the story.
• Treat the math activities as games to be played for fun.
Follow your child's lead. Spend time on those activities that
engage your child's interest and curiosity.
• Activities, especially ones using physical materials, help
make abstract mathematical ideas concrete.

Learning is a messy process. Learning about math calls for
children to become immersed in lively experiences that help
them make sense of mathematical concepts and symbols.

Although learning about numbers is basic to math, other
ideas, such as identifying shapes and patterns, measuring,
collecting and interpreting data, reasoning logically, and thinking about chance, are also important. By reading these stories
and having fun with the activities, you will help your child
enthusiastically say "**Hello, math,**" instead of "I hate math."

—Marilyn Burns
National Mathematics Educator
Author of *The I Hate Mathematics! Book*

For Rupa Basu, a whiz in math!
—J.R.

Copyright © 1998 by Scholastic Inc.
The activities on pages 43-48 copyright © 1998 by Marilyn Burns.
All rights reserved. Published by Scholastic Inc.
HELLO READER! and CARTWHEEL BOOKS and associated logos
are trademarks and/or registered trademarks of Scholastic Inc.

Library of Congress Cataloging-in-Publication Data

Rocklin, Joanne.
    The case of the backyard treasure/by Joanne Rocklin: math activities by
Marilyn Burns; illustrated by John Speirs.
        p. cm. — (Hello reader! math. Level 4)
    Summary: Liz the Whiz and her younger brother use codes, a chart, and a
map of the backyard that matches a clock face to solve Zack's mystery. Includes
a section with related activities.
    ISBN 0-590-30872-6
    [1. Mystery and detective stories. 2. Ciphers — Fiction. 3. Maps — Fiction.]
I. Burns, Marilyn. II. Speirs, John, ill. III. Title. IV. Series.
PZ7.R59Caf   1998
[E] — DC21   97-11462
                                                                        CIP
                                                                         AC

10 9 8 7 6 5 4 3 2 1   8 9/9 0/0 01 02

Printed in the U.S.A.   24
First printing, April 1998

THE CASE OF
THE BACKYARD
TREASURE

by Joanne Rocklin
Illustrated by John Speirs
Math Activities by Marilyn Burns

Hello Reader! Math — Level 4

SCHOLASTIC INC.
New York   Toronto   London   Auckland   Sydney

My name is Liz the Whiz.
This is my little brother, Henry.
He's a Whiz-in-Training (WIT).

Marv is our dog.
He's smarter than he looks.
Marv's Nose Always Knows.

Henry, Marv, and I solve problems.
We are a great team.

But every now and then
we get a hard case to crack.
Very hard.

It is the day after Henry's birthday.
He has a shiny new watch.
"1:01 P.M.," says Henry the WIT.
Marv snores.
"1:02 P.M.," Henry says.

"That's a great watch," I say. "Guess it works."
"Sure does. It will help us with our work, too,"
says Henry.

He doesn't know how right he is!

"1:03 P.M." Henry says.

Zack is racing down our street.
"Liz the Whiz!" he shouts.
"I've got a big problem!"

Everybody knows about Liz the Whiz
and Company.
I leave my card every place I go.

Got a problem?
Liz the Whiz & Co.
will solve it.

Zack is waving a piece of paper.
"Read this note quickly!" he shouts.

"Please, calm down," I say.
"We will solve your problem."

The note says…

"Strange note," I say.

"We don't have much time
to find the treasure!" Zack says.
Henry looks at his shiny new watch.
He thinks hard.
"We have fifty-five minutes, to be exact,"
Henry says.
"But where is the treasure?
And whose treasure is it?
And why do we have to find it by 2:00 P.M.?"
asks Zack.

I, Liz the Whiz, stay calm.
"I promise we will answer all your questions,"
I say.
I begin to collect the clues.
"Do you have a friend named 19-1-13?" I ask.
"No," says Zack.
"Get the Code Book," I say to Henry.

I read the note again.
"Do you have a friend who just moved away?"
I continue.
"Yes! My friend Sam!" Zack says.
I write down that fact. Then I study the
Code Book. I, Liz the Whiz, crack the code.
"It's the old Alphabet Code," I say to my partner.
Henry the WIT thinks hard.
"You mean—?" he asks.
"Yes! Let's go to Sam's backyard!" I say.

1	2	3	4	5	6	7	8	9	10
A	B	C	D	E	F	G	H	I	J

11	12	13	14	15	16	17	18	19	20
K	L	M	N	O	P	Q	R	S	T

21	22	23	24	25	26
U	V	W	X	Y	Z

We all run to Sam's backyard.
Marv sniffs around a big 20-18-5-5.
Zack has the Code Book.
"T — R . . . ," he spells out.
Henry and I are already at the big tree.
"Now we will find the treasure!" says Henry.
But he is wrong.
Very wrong.

All we find is another note.
It says…

Less than five
but more than two,
how many feet ahead
to another clue?

"I give up! This is too hard!" says Zack.
He flops down on the grass.

But my partner and I stay on the job.
"What numbers are less than five?"
I ask Henry the WIT.
"Four, three, two, one, and zero," he says.

"You are well-trained," I say.
I write down those facts.
"What numbers are more than two but less than five?" I ask.
"Three and four," says Henry.
I cross out the numbers two, one, and zero.
"We will start digging at three feet and four feet," I say.

Henry uses his feet to measure three feet.
He puts down a pebble.
Then he uses his feet to measure four feet.
He puts down another pebble.

Zack says, "Wait! Sam wrote that note to me.
My feet are bigger than your feet. I will use *my*
feet to measure three feet and four feet."
"But maybe Sam was using his *own* feet
to measure three feet and four feet!" Henry says.

"Sam's feet are bigger than mine! Whose feet do
we use?" cries Zack.
Zack flops down on the grass again.
So does Henry.

Of course I, Liz the Whiz, solve the problem.
"You are using your feet, but you are not
using your head!" I say.
I pull out my tape measure.
I measure three feet.
I dig a small hole.
No clue.
I measure four feet.
I dig another hole.
There it is!

The clue says...

I pull out my notebook.
"I will write down the facts," I say.

The answer jumps right
out at us!

RED	FOUR STRAIGHT SIDES
ROSES	
ROOF	
FLOWER BOX	
WINDOW FRAME	X
DOOR	X
SHOVEL HEAD	X

We climb up and find this clue...

The treasure is twelve.
The gate is three.
The garden is six.
And nine is the tree!

But twelve what? Three what?
Six what? Nine what?

I think and think.
Suddenly, I have a terrible thought.
I, Liz the Whiz, am stumped!
That does not happen very often.

We check the tree again.
No treasure.
We check the gate.
No treasure.

Henry picks up the shovel.
"Should I start digging up the garden?"
he asks.
"No, WIT," I say.
I sit down under the tree.
"I've got some thinking to do,"
I say.

"We don't have time to think! Start digging!"
cries Zack.
Henry checks his watch.
"We have five minutes left, to be exact,"
Henry says.
"Oh, no!" says Zack.
I stare at Henry's shiny new watch.
Of course!
"Twelve o'clock!" I shout.

Henry checks his watch again.
"You are wrong," he says. "It's just a few
seconds past 1:55 P.M."

I jump up.

"You don't understand!" I say.

"Pretend the backyard is a clock or a watch.
The gate is three o'clock!"

"You mean—?" asks Henry the WIT.

"Yes!" I say. "The garden is six o'clock!"

"And the tree is nine o'clock!" says Henry.

"Right, WIT!" I say. "And twelve o'clock is—?"

"The shed!" shout Henry and Zack.

We all run to the shed.
We find the treasure!
Marv is barking his head off.
The Nose Always Knows cookies when he
smells them.
There is a letter, too.
It says…

Dear Zack,
Congratulations!
Here are ten peanut
butter cookies.
My new address is
888 Willow Street.
My new phone number
is 555-3423.
Your Friend, 19-1-13
(Sam)

"Of course, I will share the cookies
with all of you," says Zack.
He divides them equally.
There are two cookies left over.

A car and a moving van are coming down the street.
I say to Henry, "Check your watch, WIT. We found the treasure just in time. I'll bet it's exactly 2:00 P.M."

Henry checks his watch.
I am right, of course.

"I know what you can do with those extra cookies," I say.

Case closed.

• ABOUT THE ACTIVITIES •

Thinking, reasoning, and solving problems are at the heart of doing mathematics. And the more experience children have solving mathematical problems, the more successful they will be learning mathematics.

In real life, mathematical problems do not appear as they typically do in school math textbooks, as tidy arrangements of numerical exercises or word problems that provide all the information needed, with answers that can be checked with an answer key. Solving mathematical problems in daily life most often calls for figuring out what information to use, choosing what to do with it, and deciding whether the result makes sense.

The Case of the Backyard Treasure presents a variety of mathematical problems that need to be solved in order to understand a mystery. The problems call for applying skills from several areas of the mathematics curriculum—number, logic, measurement, and geometry. The story models for children how to solve problems, and the activities that follow offer additional mathematical challenges for children to tackle. Enjoy these activities and have fun being a mathematical problem solver with your child!

—Marilyn Burns

You'll find tips and suggestions for guiding the activities whenever you see a box like this!

Retelling the Story

Five notes in the story gave Liz the Whiz and Company clues about where to search for the back-yard treasure.

Zack brought the first note to Liz and Henry. It was signed, "Your Friend, 19-1-13." Liz used the Code Book to figure out that 19-1-13 was Sam. How did Liz figure this out?

Liz also figured out that 20-18-5-5 was the tree in Sam's backyard. How did she know this?

The second note was attached to the tree in Sam's yard. What did it say? How did Liz and Henry figure out that the next clue would be buried three or four feet away?

When Liz dug four feet from the tree, she found the third note. What did it say? How did Liz figure out that the next clue was in the flower box?

Liz was stumped by the fourth note, but when she stared at Henry's shiny new watch, she got a clue. How did Henry's watch help Liz figure out that they should look in the shed for the treasure?

The fifth note was in the shed. What did it say?

Liz, Henry, Zack, and Marv divided up the ten peanut butter cookies. There were two cookies left over. How many cookies did they each get?

More Alphabet Codes

If you were using the Alphabet Code, how would you write your name? How would you write Liz? Henry? Zack? Marv?

What does this message say?

9   12-9-11-5   9-3-5   3-18-5-1-13   4-15 25-15-21?

Write a message for someone else to figure out.

Other Alphabet Codes

Suppose you used a backward alphabet code, so a = 26, b = 25, c = 24, . . . and z = 1. How would you write your name? What about Liz? Henry? Zack? Marv?

What does this backward alphabet message say?

24-12-23-22-8   26-9-22   21-6-13!

Try to invent another Alphabet Code for writing secret messages.

Clues for Four Feet

The second clue in the story helped Liz figure out that the third clue was buried four feet away. Explain why each of the clues below would also lead Liz to dig four feet away.

Three more than five, divide by two.

Take seven from eight, then add on three.

Start with half a dozen, then take away two.

Can you figure out other clues for getting to four?

How Many Feet?

Figure out how many feet away Liz would have to dig for these clues.

Count all of your fingers, then take away four.

Add two and four and six, then take away five.

Add eight and four, then add on four more.

Take half of twenty, then take away eight.

Problems like these give your child valuable practice with figuring mentally. If your child is interested, make up others to solve.

Shape Clues

Match each shape with a clue.

Clue #1: I have no corners at all.

Clue #2: I have four sides and four corners and all of my corners are square.

Clue #3: I have eight sides and look like a stop sign.

Clue #4: I have four sides that are all the same length.

Clue #5: I have three corners and the same number of sides.

Draw more shapes and make up clues for them.